Field Trip to the
MOON

JOHN HARE
JEANNE WILLIS

MACMILLAN CHILDREN'S BOOKS

We saw them land in rocky sand...

. . . All sealed in silver suits.
Hand in hand, the earthlings marched
With space dust on their boots.

They parked their tiny spaceship, bright and shiny as the sun.
And speaking in a squeak, they marched behind the tallest one.

In silent fear we watched them on their field trip to the Moon.
We hid, afraid to say hello in case it was too soon.

They stayed in groups for safety
- all but one who stood apart.
And . . .

...With sticks of many colours, made a stunning work of art.
Colours, oh so wonderful, that we had never seen.
We live our lives in shades of grey, not yellow, blue and green.

Then to our great alarm,
the Earthling made a zizzing sound.
Its head drooped as it dropped
the pretty sticks upon
the ground.

z z z

Zeeki said, "It's snoring. It's what sleeping earthlings do."

But when it woke...

... The spaceship had departed
with its crew!

The Earthling ran and whirled
its arms and with a frowny face...

. . . It called, "Come back!" Alas, its words got lost in outer space.

All alone and far from home, it sat down in despair.
It looked so sad, we didn't like to leave it sitting there.

It sighed and shed a tear, which we saw with x-ray eyes.
"We have to save it!" Zeeki cried, but then to our surprise...

...It gave the bravest smile and with the green stick in its hand,
It drew a many-coloured shape we did not understand.

We crept up very quietly,
as quickly as we dared.

We called our friends to come
and see and not to be so scared.

Then Zeeki sneezed and to our shock . . .

... the Earthling span around.
It saw us...

... So we hid behind a rock without a sound.

It said, "Hello," and, "Do you like this rainbow that I drew?" And we replied, "It's beautiful..."

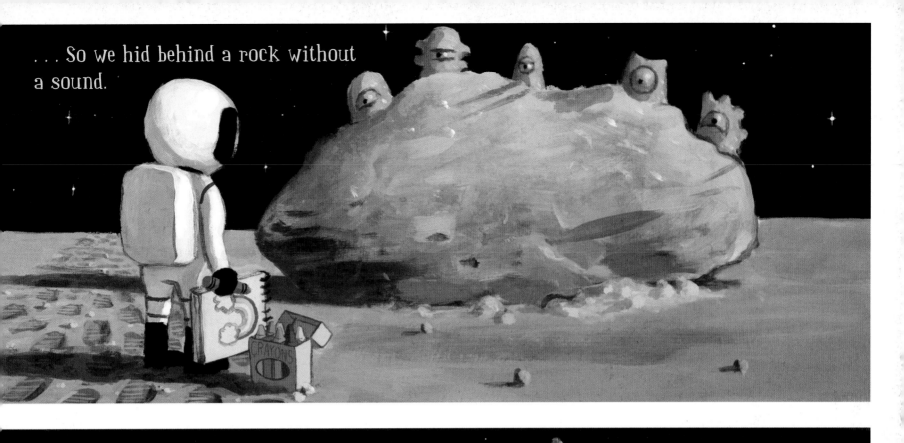

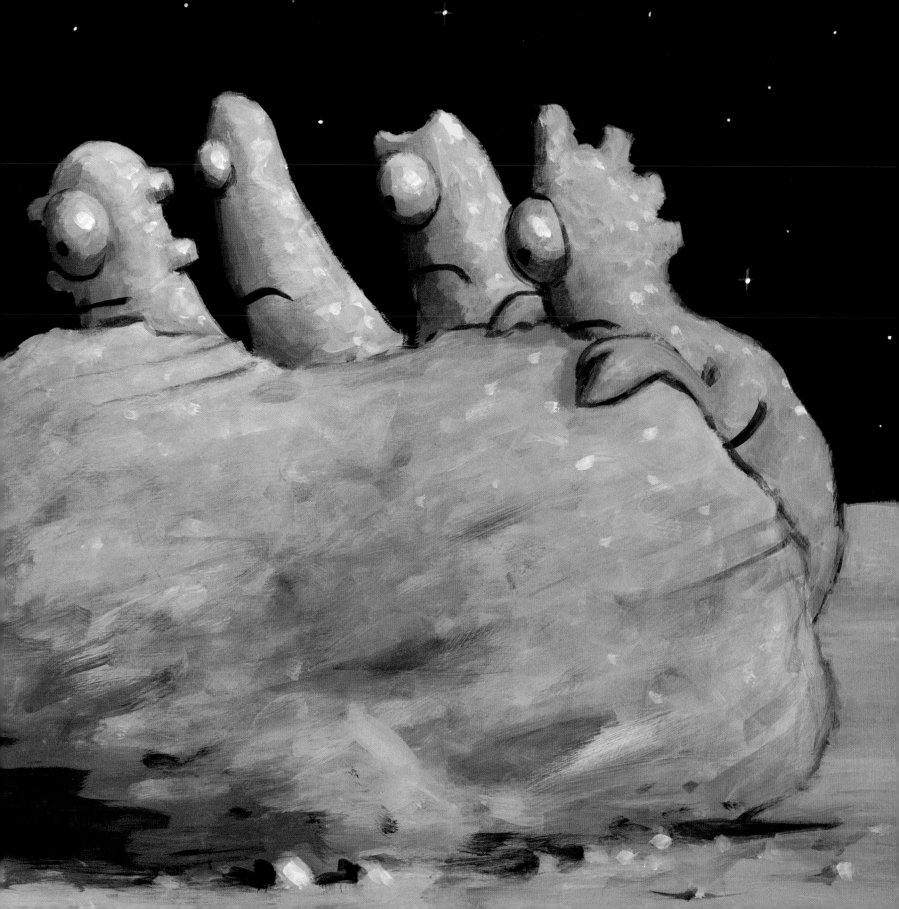

we drew on one another and the Earthling laughed like mad.
And offered us more coloured sticks and paper from a pad.

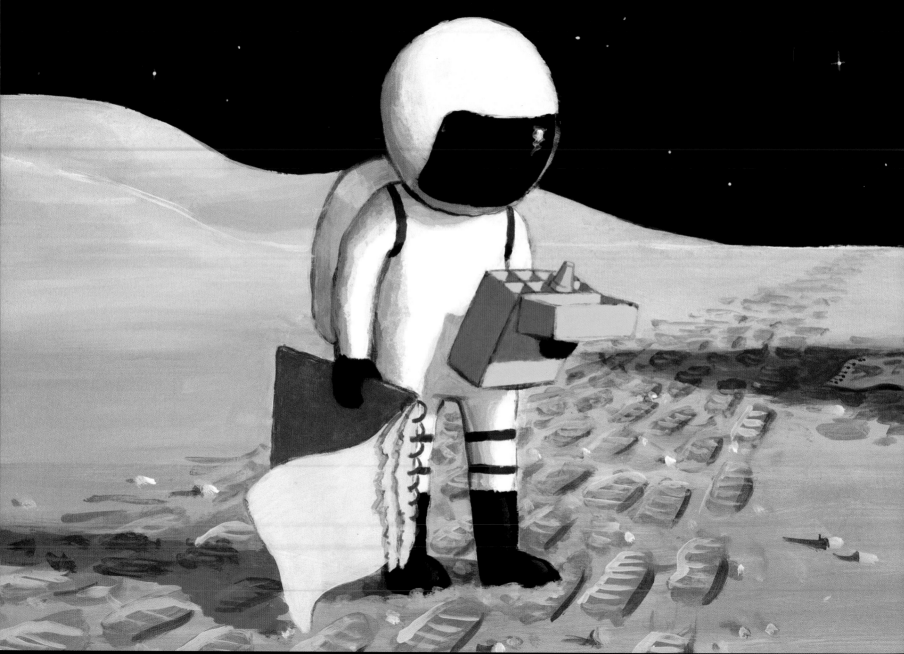

... But in the afternoon,
The shiny spaceship shuttled
back and landed on the Moon.

The Earthling looked so happy now that it was safe and sound.

But the leader wasn't pleased with all the scribbles that he found!
"It wasn't me," the Earthling said. "The aliens drew those."

"There's no such thing!" the leader said, "As everybody knows."
"Clean it up at once!" he said. "Don't leave a trace behind."
But...

... The Earthling left its rainbow colours in our hearts and minds.